The Brave Little Tailor

illustrated by Laura Barella

Child's Play (International) Ltd
Ashworth Rd, Bridgemead, Swindon, SN5 7YD UK
Swindon   Auburn ME   Sydney
© 2014 Child's Play (International) Ltd   Printed in Guangzhou, China
ISBN 978-1-84643-654-3   Z030114FUFT04146543
1 3 5 7 9 10 8 6 4 2
www.childs-play.com

One summer morning, a little tailor was sewing a new jacket for one of his customers. He was feeling hungry, so he made a slice of bread and honey. "I'll have that when I've finished," he thought, and put the plate to one side. But the smell of the honey attracted a swarm of flies, and they were hungry too!

"Hey!" shouted the little tailor. "Get off my bread!"
But the flies carried on eating his bread and honey.
He grabbed a length
of cloth and waved
it wildly at them.

When he had finished, there were seven dead flies lying on his bread.

"I'm so brave!" he said. "It's a shame there was no one else here to see it. I'll have to make sure everyone knows!" And he cut out a banner, and embroidered on it: SEVEN WITH ONE BLOW. He tied it around his middle and set off, grabbing a lump of cheese as he went.

As he walked along the road, he came across a bird caught in a bush. He freed it, and put it into his pocket along with the cheese.

The road led up a
mountain, and there
he found a tall giant.
"Good day!" he said.
"Look at me!
I'm really strong!"
And he showed the
giant his banner.

SEVEN WITH
ONE BLOW

"You really killed seven soldiers with a single blow?!" asked the giant, disbelievingly. "I'll bet you aren't strong enough to do this, though!" And she picked up a stone in one hand, and squeezed it until water dripped out!
The brave little tailor thought quickly. He pulled the lump of soft cheese out of his pocket, and squeezed it between his fingers.
"Easy!" he crowed. "What else have you got?"

"This!" answered the giant.
She picked up a stone
and threw it so high into the
air that it was lost to sight.
They waited and waited,
until the stone finally fell
back to earth.

"Not bad," said the tailor, "but I can throw this stone so high that it will NEVER fall back to earth!" And he pulled the bird out of his pocket and threw it in the air. The bird was delighted to be set free, and flew up and away, and never came back.

"Not bad. But are you strong enough to carry a whole tree?" asked the giant. "Of course!" answered the clever tailor. "You go first, and I'll carry the rest of the tree behind you." As soon as the giant turned her back, the brave little tailor jumped onto the tree, and let the giant carry him along.

Soon, the giant became tired. The tailor jumped off, pretending that he had been carrying the tree all the time.

"I'll bet you can't do this!" bragged the giant. She grabbed a cherry tree by the top branch, and bent it over until it touched the ground. The little tailor grabbed hold of it too, but as soon as the giant let go, the cherry tree sprang upright again, throwing the tailor through the air. "See?" laughed the giant. "You can't even hold down a cherry tree!" "I was jumping over it," explained the tailor. "I bet you can't!"

The giant leapt as high as she could. But she couldn't clear the tree, and she became tangled in the branches.

The giant was cross because the little tailor was better and stronger at everything. She decided to take him to her home and kill him.
"You can have my bed," the giant said to the tailor. "Sleep well!"
But the bed was too large, so the tailor slept on the floor. In the middle of the night, the giant crept up and chopped the bed with a huge knife.

The giant was amazed to see the tailor alive the next morning. "I thought you were dead!" she gasped. "No," said the tailor. "Just a bit tired!"

"He's more than a match for me!" said the giant to her friends. "Let's get out of here before he wants revenge!"

The brave little tailor went on his way, until he
came to a castle. The king welcomed him in.
"You killed seven soldiers with one blow?"
he asked. "You must be strong and brave.
Will you join my army?"

But the king's soldiers did not like the tailor, and threatened to leave. So the king decided to send the tailor to fight two dangerous giants who would certainly kill him.
"If you succeed," he lied, "I will give you half my kingdom!"

The brave little tailor soon found the two giants, who were fast asleep. He climbed a tree and dropped a stone onto one of them. The giant woke up, furious.
"Why are you hitting me?" he asked the other.
"I'm not," came the reply.
"Go back to sleep."
As soon as they were both asleep again, the little tailor threw more rocks, this time onto the other giant.

The giants argued again, and this time they started fighting. Neither of them would give in, and they started hitting each other with trees, until they both fell down dead!

Now the tailor returned to claim his reward,
but the king did not wish to keep his promise.
"There is one more challenge you must complete,"
he said. "In the woods there is a unicorn.
Many have tried to capture it without success."
"No problem!" replied the tailor, and he set off
at once.

The unicorn was frightened, and charged at the tailor, who was standing in front of a tree. But he jumped to one side, so that the creature's horn became stuck in the trunk. Gently, the tailor freed the unicorn, and led it back to the castle.

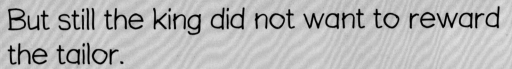

But still the king did not want to reward
the tailor.
"How can I get out of my promise?" he
thought. "I want all my riches for myself!"
Gathering together some of his strongest
soldiers, he hatched a plan to capture the
tailor and send him far away. But the king's
squire overheard them plotting, and told
the tailor.

That night, the tailor was waiting for the soldiers behind the bedroom door. He stood in front of a light, so that it spread a huge shadow. "I'm afraid of no one," he said. "I've killed seven with one blow, got the better of giants, and captured a magic unicorn. Anyone who tries to double-cross me would be very foolish." The soldiers were so scared, they ran off into the night.

"Goodbye!" called the tailor. "Now I'll just find the king and make him keep his promise!"

Trembling, the king led the tailor to his treasure. Happily, the tailor helped himself to exactly half. "The people in my village can eat properly now," he smiled. "And I'll be able to make lovely clothes for all of them. And all because I killed seven flies!" The king gasped. "All you killed was seven flies?" "Of course," laughed the tailor. "What on earth did you think I killed, just with one blow?!"